This book is dedicated to Beavers, who are the fastest and the best builders in the world; and especially to the new Beavers of Scotland, who have just moved back in after many years away. Good luck, Beavers!

First published 2011 by Walker Books Ltd
87 Vauxhall Walk, London SE11 5HJ

10 9 8 7 6 5 4 3 2 1

© 2011 Inga Moore

The right of Inga Moore to be identified as author/illustrator of this work has been asserted by her in accordance with the Copyright, Designs and Patents Act 1988

This book has been typeset in Clarendon T

Printed in China

British Library Cataloguing in Publication Data:
a catalogue record for this book is available
from the British Library

ISBN 978-1-4063-2432-7

www.walker.co.uk

A House in the Woods

INGA MOORE

WALKER BOOKS
AND SUBSIDIARIES
LONDON · BOSTON · SYDNEY · AUCKLAND

A Little Pig had made a den for herself
in the woods. Next door another Little Pig
had made himself a hut.

One morning the two Little Pigs
went out walking together.
One Little Pig found a feather
and the other found an
interesting stick.

But when the first Little Pig brought her feather
home to her den, she discovered Bear had moved in –
which she didn't mind, because she liked Bear.

Only Bear was so big – oh dear!
The den was wrecked.

And when the second Little Pig went home to his hut with his stick, he discovered Moose had moved in – which he didn't mind either, because he liked Moose.

Only Moose was even bigger than Bear, and when he stood up politely to say good morning – CRASH! The hut was also wrecked.

Which left the two Little Pigs with nowhere
to live – not to mention Moose and Bear –
and this was a pickle, it really was.

Then Moose had a brilliant idea – why not build
a big house where they could all live together?

Well, it was an exciting plan!
Except that building a big house
with real windows and doors,
a roof, stairs and chimney stacks,
isn't easy. They couldn't do it
on their own.

So Moose called the Beavers
on the telephone ...

and soon afterwards a team of Beaver Builders
came to help them with the work.

The Beavers said, if it was all right, they wished
to be paid in peanut butter sandwiches –
to which no one had any objection.

So they felled the timber ...

and the work began.

By lunch-time the walls
of the house were up ...

and by tea time the roof was on.
*(The lunch and tea times were
on different days, of course.
Beavers are fast, but not
that fast.)*

Bear made the staircases and
chimney stacks, while Moose
fitted the windows and doors.

Then they both went with the two Little Pigs
to the junkyard for furniture and curtains
and all those things that go inside a house.

At last the house was finished.

The Beavers handed over their bill and left.

There was just enough time to get to the store ...

to buy the bread and peanut butter.

Then the Little Pigs helped Moose and Bear
make six plates of peanut butter sandwiches,

which they delivered in person to the Beavers
who had all gone back to their lodge on the lake.

It had been a busy time for the Little Pigs and Moose and Bear.

They had worked hard, especially Bear.

Had it been worth it?

What do you think?

Just look!
What a beautiful new house they had to go home to!

Bear went to bed first
because she was so tired.
And after they had finished
their supper and washed
the dishes ...

and told stories for a while round the fire,
it was the turn of Moose and the two Little Pigs
to climb the stairs to bed.

Soon the only sounds to be
heard were the soft cheeps
of sleepy birds roosting in
the rafters; and the tiny
rustling of woodmice in
the fallen leaves outside;
and, just now and then,
the gentle snoring of Bear.

Good night, Bear.
Good night, Moose.
Good night, Little Pigs.

Sweet dreams, everyone!